This Little Tiger book belongs to:

_____

_____

_____

_____

FOR ALISON LOWE
WITH LOVE
~C.P.

FOR JULIA AND VICKY
WITH LOVE
~J.C.

LITTLE TIGER PRESS
An imprint of Magi Publications
1 The Coda Centre, 189 Munster Road,
London SW6 6AW, UK
www.littletigerpress.com

First published in Great Britain 1998 by
Little Tiger Press, London
This edition published 2008

2 4 6 8 10 9 7 5 3

Don't Be Afraid, Little One

CAROLINE PITCHER

ILLUSTRATED BY
JANE CHAPMAN

LITTLE TIGER PRESS

One moonlit night, while the wind
raged and the rain drummed on the stable
roof, a foal was born. His mother the mare
breathed on him softly, until he struggled
up on a tangle of long legs.

"What's that noise?" asked the foal.
"Just the wind," answered the mare,
nuzzling his velvety neck.
"Where is the wind?"
"It's blowing in the hills," replied
his mother. "When you are big and
your legs aren't wobbly anymore,
you will run with the wind
over the hills."
"Will you be there with me?" asked
the foal.
"No," said his mother. "But you
won't think of me then."

The foal didn't like his mother saying that. "Why won't I think of you?" he asked.

His mother sighed and shook her long black mane. "Because you won't. Now settle down, little one. No more questions."

"What are questions?" yawned the foal, and then he fell fast asleep.

Spring came, and the foal's legs
grew longer and stronger, so that
his head just reached the top of
the stable door.
"What's outside?" he asked.
"It's a field," said the mare. "Soon
you will be able to go there with
me and run all the way around
and back again."
"I don't think I want to," said
the foal, drawing back. "I don't
like Outside. I like it here."

The foal's legs grew even stronger and longer. Now he could see right over the stable door. He saw other horses.

There was a great shire horse with giant hooves, and a tiny Shetland pony with very long hair. He saw a horse as dark as the night sky, and a pony as pale as moonlight. "Where are their mothers?" he asked. "Some of them are here and some are at other stables," said the mare. "They give people rides. I'll soon do that, too, little one, while you stay behind."

Stay behind!

"No," said the foal, turning his back.
"I don't want to think about it."

When the days grew warmer,
the mare and her foal went out
into the field. They ran all the
way around it and back again.

Twilight fell, and the foal became uneasy.

"Can't we go back to the stable now?" he asked.

"No," said his mother. "When the nights are warm, we stay outside."

"But it's *dark*!"

"It's dark in the stable, too, little one. It's the same dark."

"It's not such a big dark there," said the foal.

"I can't see you out here when you move away from me. I'm all alone."

"You know I'm here, even if you can't see me," whispered the mare.

The foal lifted his head in the darkness.
"What's making that noise?" he asked.
"Just the wind. Don't you remember
hearing it when you were very small?"
"Yes," said the foal. "But where is it?"
"You know it's there, but you can't see it."
"Just like you in the dark, Mom," he
whispered.

One morning, the foal woke late. He had done so much running and growing the day before he was very tired. But where was his mother? The foal looked inside the stable, but she wasn't there. Then he saw her by the fence. She had a bridle over her head and a saddle on her back.

"I'm going back to work," she called to him. "I'm going to give rides again."

"And who will ride me?" cried the foal with excitement.

"You're too little to be ridden yet," explained his mother. "Your back is weak, your mouth is soft as silk, and your legs would snap like twigs."

"But I'll be all alone," he wailed. "Oh, please stay with me!"

"No," said the mare, as a little girl climbed
on to her back. "You'll be just fine."
The foal watched as his mother and her
rider trotted out of sight. He was all alone.
"Come back, Mom!" he neighed, and his
voice echoed in the hills.

He heard something answer
him, but it wasn't his mother.
It was the wind!
The wind had come down from the
hills to play with him. It blew in his
mane and his tail, and it blew in the
trees and stirred all the leaves. It blew
a butterfly for the foal to chase, and
it blew a path in the meadow that he
could run right through. It even blew
waves in the water of his
drinking trough.

The foal jumped and ran and
bucked and chased and flicked
his little black tail. He ran with
the wind all morning.

And then, just as the foal was too tired to run and jump anymore, his mother came back. She nuzzled his neck and said, "You see—nothing bad happened to you when you were alone."

Oh my, thought the foal. I was having so much fun I didn't think of Mom once.

"I wasn't alone," he said. "The wind played with me."

"So you didn't think of me at all?"

"Well, maybe a *little* bit," said the foal.

"That's good," said the mare. "I was thinking of you the whole time!"

fantastic reads from Little Tiger Press

THE LONG JOURNEY HOME
David Bedford and Penny Ives

Rosie's Special Surprise
Julia Rawlinson   Tim Warnes

SLEEP TIGHT, GINGER KITTEN
Adèle Geras
Catherine Walters

Don't be so nosy, Posy!
Nicola Grant
illustrated by
Tim Warnes

Sleepy Sam
Michael Catchpool
illustrated by
Eleanor Taylor

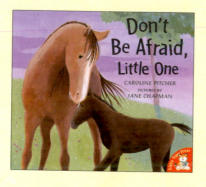

Don't Be Afraid, Little One
CAROLINE PITCHER
PICTURES BY
JANE CHAPMAN

Michael Coleman
Tim Warnes
George & Sylvia
A Tale of True Love

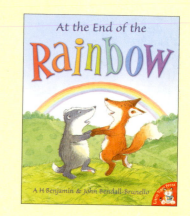

At the End of the Rainbow
A H Benjamin & John Bendall-Brunello

for information regarding any of the above titles
or for our catalogue, please contact us:
Little Tiger Press, 1 The Coda Centre,
189 Munster Road, London SW6 6AW, UK
Tel: +44 (0)20 7385 6333 fax: +44 (0)20 7385 7333
E-mail: info@littletiger.co.uk
www.littletigerpress.com

Clever Little Freddy
Christine Leeson
Joanne Moss

One, Two, Three, Oops!
Michael Coleman
Gwyneth Williamson